Little Red Riding Hood

Copyright © QEB Publishing, Inc. 2004

Published in the United States by
QEB Publishing, Inc.
23062 La Cadena Drive
Laguna Hills
Irvine
CA 92653

Library of Congress Control Number 2004102067

ISBN 1-59566-020-8

Written by Anne Faundez
Designed by Alix Wood
Editor Hannah Ray
Illustrated by Elisa Squillace

Series Consultant Anne Faundez
Creative Director Louise Morley
Editorial Manager Jean Coppendale

Printed and bound in China

Little Red Riding Hood

Anne Faundez

QEB Publishing, Inc.

Once upon a time, there was a little girl who lived in a village near the woods. Her name was Little Red Riding Hood.

Do you know why she was called Little Red Riding Hood? It was because she had a beautiful red cloak with a hood, made by her granny.

The girl was very proud of her cloak and she wore it all the time. So everyone called her Little Red Riding Hood.

One day, Little Red Riding Hood's granny was sick in bed. Little Red Riding Hood helped her mother bake a cake for her granny.

"Little Red Riding Hood, take the cake to your granny. Hurry up, now. Come home before the sun goes down, and don't talk to strangers," said Little Red Riding Hood's mother.

Little Red Riding Hood put the cake in a basket and set off for her granny's cottage, on the other side of the woods.

Granny's House

The sun was high in the sky, and sunlight filled the woods. Birds sang in the trees and little creatures bustled to and fro across the path. Little Red Riding Hood was very happy.

In the distance, Little Red Riding Hood saw a glade full of bright blue and pink flowers. She wandered off the path toward them. Granny will love these flowers, she thought. She picked some flowers and then continued on her way. By this time, the sun was low in the sky.

9

Suddenly, she heard a noise.
A scuffling, shuffling noise.
A big gray wolf stood in front of her.
   "Where are you going?" he asked.
   "I'm going to visit my granny.
She lives on the other
side of the woods and
she's not very well,"
replied Little Red
Riding Hood.

Little Red Riding Hood
had forgotten that her
mother told her not to
speak to strangers.

"I'd like to visit her, too," said the wolf. "You know what? You go your way and I'll take another path."
The wolf took a short cut.
Little Red Riding Hood continued on her way.

Now and then, Little Red Riding Hood stopped to pick more flowers. By now, the sun had set and the woods were filled with shadows.

The wolf arrived at Granny's house. He rapped on the door. Knock.Knock.

"Who's there?" asked Granny.

"Little Red Riding Hood," replied the wolf, in a squeaky voice.

"Lift the latch, my dear, and come in," said Granny.

The wolf bounded into the room.
He yanked the old lady out
of bed and bundled her
into a closet.

He jumped into her bed and
pulled the blankets up to his chin.

Little Red Riding Hood
arrived at her granny's
house. She rapped on
the door.
Knock. Knock.
  "Who's there?" said
a voice.
  "Little Red Riding
Hood," she answered.
  "Lift the latch, my
dear, and come in,"
called the voice.

Now, Little Red Riding Hood had never seen her granny sick in bed. She was surprised.

"Granny, what BIG arms you've got!" she said.

"All the better to hug you with, my dear," said the wolf.

17

"Granny, what BIG ears you've got!" she said.
"All the better to hear you with, my dear," said the wolf.
"Granny, what BIG eyes you've got!" she said.

"All the better to see you with, my dear," said the wolf.
"Granny, what BIG teeth you've got!" she said.
"All the better to EAT you with, my dear!"

And the wolf jumped out of bed and chased
Little Red Riding Hood around the room.

Just at that moment, by the light of the moon, a woodcutter was passing by. He heard a terrible banging and clanging coming from the cottage. He rushed inside and chased that wicked wolf right out of the woods and far away.

Little Red Riding Hood thanked the woodcutter. Then she unpacked her basket, and Granny, the woodcutter, and Little Red Riding Hood sat down to a feast of cake. And they all lived happily ever after.

What do you think?

Which words would you use to describe Little Red Riding Hood?

Where does the wolf put Granny?

What does the wolf say about his BIG teeth?

Who chases away the wolf? What might the wolf be thinking?

23

Carers' and teachers' notes

- Look at the cover. Ask your child to talk about the picture. Does he/she recognize the little girl?
- Read the title together. Tell your child that the title is the name of the story.
- Explain that Little Red Riding Hood is a traditional tale, which means that it's a story that has been passed down, from generation to generation, by word of mouth. Explain that there is no correct way of telling the story, and that it exists in many different versions. As each person retells it, he or she often brings in a new element to the story.
- Tell your child that traditional tales usually begin with "Once upon a time" and usually end with "And they all lived happily ever after."
- Explain that traditional stories usually contain a moral, which teaches us something.
- Talk about the moral in this story. Can your child guess what it is? (Never talk to strangers.)
- Explain that traditional stories often have a speaking animal as a character. Other typical characters are princes, princesses, kings, queens, wise old people, wizards, and magicians. Can your child think of other stories that feature any of these characters?
- Point out any words and phrases that move the story along and show the passing of time. E.g. "now and then," "by now" and "by this time."
- Can your child suggest why the word "BIG" on pages 17, 18, and 19 is written in capitals? (For emphasis.)
- Have fun reading the wolf's speeches, using appropriate voices for when he first meets Little Red Riding Hood, and when he is pretending to be Granny.
- Together, write down some ideas for a traditional story. Make a list of the characters that will appear in your story? What will the moral of your story be?
- Together, draft your story, using the opening "Once upon a time" and the ending "And they all lived happily ever after." Encourage your child to draw some pictures to accompany his/her story.